PENGUIN YOUNG READERS LICENSES

An imprint of Penguin Random House LLC, New York

First published in Australia by Puffin Books, 2021

First published in the United States of America by Penguin Young Readers Licenses,
an imprint of Penguin Random House LLC, New York, 2023

This book is based on the TV series *Bluey*.

BLUEY™ and BLUEY character logos ™ & © Ludo Studio Pty Ltd 2018.
Licensed by BBC Studios. BBC logo ™ & © BBC 1996.

Visit us online at penguinrandomhouse.com.

Manufactured in China

ISBN 9780593659588   10 9 8 7 6 5 4 3 2 1 HH

The publisher does not have any control over and does not assume any responsibility
for author or third-party websites or their content.

It's sleepytime at the Heeler house. Bingo is on her second book with Mum, while Bluey is already fast asleep.

Now it's time for lights out. Bingo wants to do a Big Girl sleep and wake up in her own bed.

"Sweet dreams," Mum says. "Remember, I'm always here if you need me."

Bingo holds Floppy close and drifts off to sleep.

She begins to dream.

Bingo sees a big, warm, glowing light.

They head towards it. On the way, they pass another planet.
Someone else has already hatched from this one.

I WONDER WHO?

Bingo and Floppy head off into space again. Oooooh . . . a planet!

This one looks cozy.

It **IS** cozy!

BOOMP!

Bingo and Floppy feel like they're rolling up and down big blue space mountains.

It's a lot of fun.

Then they find another planet—the biggest one yet.

This one is a lot
of fun to jump on . . .

So much fun
that Bluey joins in.

Not much fun
for Dad, though.

They all end up back in Mum and Dad's room.

The blanket slips off.

Bingo and Floppy are left shivering in the cold.

Bingo spots that warm, glowing light again.

On their way towards the light, they pass another planet. This one has something spinning around it—it's Floppy's friends! Floppy wants to join them.

Bingo lets Floppy go.

Wait, what's this? Something's heading towards Bingo!

WHOOSH!

But Bingo remembers that she wants to do a Big Girl sleep and wake up in her own bed.

Bingo stands up.

I HAVE TO GO . . . I'm a BIG GIRL nOW.

REMEMBER, I'LL ALWAYS BE HERE FOR YOU.

EVEN IF YOU CAN'T SEE ME.

Because I love you.

Bingo floats back to where she began . . .

. . . but she can't fit all the pieces together.

HOORAY! Here comes Floppy with her friends to help.

NIGHT NIGHT, BINGO.

NIGHT, FLOPPY. THANKS FOR EVERYTHING.

The Heeler house is still and quiet again. Bingo sleeps peacefully.

Dad and Bluey sleep peacefully.

Mum does, too.

The sun begins to rise. Its rays warm Bingo.

Asleep in her own bed.